THE MATCHLOCK GUN

THE
MATCHLOCK
GUN

By Walter D. Edmonds

Illustrated by Paul Lantz

The Putnam & Grosset Group

Printed on recycled paper

A PaperStar Book, published in 1998 by Penguin Putnam Books
for Young Readers, 345 Hudson Street, New York, NY 10014.
PaperStar is a registered trademark of The Putnam Berkley Group, Inc.
The PaperStar logo is a trademark of The Putnam Berkley Group, Inc.
Published in 1989 by G. P. Putnam's Sons.
Originally published in 1941 by Dodd, Mead & Co., Inc.
Published simultaneously in Canada.
Printed in the United States of America.

Library of Congress Cataloging-in-Publication Data
Edmonds, Walter Dumaux, 1903-1998. The matchlock gun.
Summary: In 1756, during the French and Indian War in upper
New York State, ten-year-old Edward is determined to protect his
home and family with the ancient, and much too heavy, Spanish gun
that his father had given him before leaving home to fight the enemy.
1. United States—French and Indian War, 1755-1763—Juvenile fiction.
[United States—French and Indian war, 1755-1763—Fiction.
2. Frontier and pioneer life—New York (State)—Fiction.
3. Courage—Fiction] I. Lantz, Paul, 1908- ill. II. Title.
PZ7.E247Mat 1989 [Fic] 88-32471
ISBN 0-698-11680-1

30 29 28 27 26 25

To my Godson

Nicholas Biddle Edmonds

FOREWORD

✦ ✦ ✦ ✦ ✦

PERHAPS you would like to know the rest of
the lullaby that Gertrude Van Alstyne sings in
this story. It is a real old Dutch song, and lots of
mothers sang it to their children up and down
the Hudson Valley and in and around Albany
in 1757, when New York State was still a British
Colony, when the French were still leading

Indians out of Canada against the settlers, and when the raid that came all the way to Guilderland, just outside of Albany City, took place.

This is the way the song goes:

> *"Trip a trop a troenje;*
> *De varken en de boenjen,*
> *De koejen en de klaver,*
> *De paardje en de haver,*
> *De kalfje en de langen gras,*
> *De eenjen en de vater-plas;*
> *So groet myn klynen pappetje vas."*

and this also is the translation:

"Up and down on a little throne; (Mother's or Father's knee)
   The pigs are in the beans,
   The cows are in the clover,
   The colts are in the stable,
   The calf is in the long grass,

The ducks are in the pond;
So big my little baby was."

The Van Alstynes were real people. Teunis was a Dutchman, as most of the early settlers round Albany were. His wife, Gertrude, was a Palatine, which meant that her people originally came from the small states, called the Palatinate, along the upper part of the River Rhine in Germany. Their lands were devastated by war; they were politically persecuted by both French and Germans; and they left their homes, going first to Holland, then to England, and finally coming to America, because they wanted to be free. They mingled well with the Dutch—except for a few crusty specimens like the Widow Van Alstyne, who felt contempt for anyone who happened to be very poor. There were plenty of others, like Teunis for instance, who knew better.

You may think it odd that the story of this raid in Guilderland should have been preserved down to the present day because of plump Trudy, and not through anything Edward ever did. Trudy became known as the greatest and best spinster in the Helderbergs. Even after she married and became Trudy Hogle she was still known as the best spinster. A spinster is someone who spins. Because her mother's shoulder was crippled by the Indian's tomahawk, Trudy was taught to spin at the age of six, and was soon good enough to do all the spinning for her family. She became so unusually good, and her spinning was so unusually fine, that her descendants told their children about Trudy Hogle from generation to generation, and that was how her great-great-great-grandson (whose name is Thomas R. Shepherd, and who lives in Ilion, New York) came to know about Trudy and about Edward and the Indians and the Spanish Gun.

It was not unusual to find Spanish guns in Holland, for the Spaniards had once invaded that country and believed they had conquered it. That is something no one should believe, for the Dutch are never good at staying beaten. In fact when you say, "Doesn't that beat the Dutch?" you mean, "Isn't that just about incredible?"

As a matter of fact, the Palatine Germans had a bit of the same peculiarity, and so did the Pilgrims, and the Scotch-Irish, and the English, whether they caught it from the Dutch, who have always suffered from the complaint, or whether it is born in every man and woman who wants to be free, to think as he chooses, and to live as he likes, and who means to do so, too.

Walter D. Edmonds

CONTENTS

✦ ✦ ✦ ✦ ✦

Foreword   vii

CHAPTER

I. The Spanish Gun   1

II. In the Loft   10

III. The Small Fields   15

IV. Indian Fires   19

V. Loading the Gun   26

VI. Edward's Orders   33

VII. Indians on the Farm   35

VIII. "Ateoord!"   39

IX. Firing the Gun   44

X. The Militia Return   49

I: THE SPANISH GUN

✦ ✦ ✦ ✦ ✦

EDWARD watched intently as his father struggled into the blue uniform coat that he had had made when he was elected captain of the Guilderland militia. It was a fine thing, he thought, to have Captain Teunis Van Alstyne for one's father, but he did wish that some day, just once even, his father would take the Spanish Gun to the muster.

It hung over the fireplace, its bell mouth pointing towards the front of the house, its brass-heeled stock towards the shed door. It was longer than a grown man, half again the length of the musket kept on pegs over the stoop door, and more than twice the length of Edward, who was ten years old, with long legs, dark hair, like his mother's, and serious eyes.

Teunis Van Alstyne often said that he had seen culverins that did not look so big as this matchlock gun. He used to tease Gertrude, his wife, about it, asking whether she had brought the gun with her to kill Indians. They were a young couple to have a ten-year-old son; they were handsome and high-spirited; he, lusty and thick-set, a true Dutchman; she, showing her Palatine breeding, dark, brown-eyed, with black hair braided round her head, her slim body limber and quick about her work. They had been nineteen and sixteen when they married; and she hated it when Teunis put on the militia coat.

All summer he had been going off on military service, into the hills and down to Albany; and every time, to Edward's disappointment, he took the musket.

This time, before Teunis could reach for it, Edward asked, "Aren't you ever going to take the big gun, Father?"

Teunis swung round to his son, looking down into the thin serious dark face. "Look, Edward, I'll show you." He lifted the long gun down. It was so heavy that a man could hardly hold it. As for Edward, when he tried, he could not keep both ends off the floor together.

Then, as though Van Aernam were not waiting outside impatiently in the gathering darkness, sitting his own horse and holding Teunis's mare, Teunis bent down to show the boy how the gun worked. "See, Edward (he pronounced the name *Ateoord* in the Dutch manner), it's a matchlock. It doesn't fire itself like the musket, with a flint. You have got to touch the priming with fire, like a cannon. It's a nonsensical, old-fashioned kind of a gun, isn't it?"

Edward felt disappointment over the lock. But he still thought it was a magnificent gun; and the candlelight caught the tracery on the brass bindings, making them look rich. He let go of it reluctantly when his father straightened up to replace it over the fireplace. Gertrude stooped down to pat her son. "Never mind," she said to him, "your Great-Grandfather Dygert brought it all the way over from Holland with him."

Edward brightened a little. "Yes," he cried, "he bought it in Bergom op Zoom to bring to the wild America."

Six-year-old Trudy laughed and said, "Bergom op Zoom!" and clapped her hands and jumped up and down in delight.

Teunis took his hat from his wife and looked at her over the heads of their children. Outside one of the horses jingled its bits as it shook itself. A northwest rain was falling, a real

November storm that had been blowing all day over the Helderbergs, with low clouds driving. At dusk, just before Van Aernam came, they had heard geese quartering the clouds, invisible and high. Winter was coming close.

"Where are you going, Teunis?"

"To Palatine Bridge."

"Did Van Aernam say whether there were any French?"

She was stuffing half a loaf and some sausage into his pouch, but she was looking at him. He had taken down the musket. He looked so manly and brave in his blue coat with red facings, his wide-brim hat and heavy boots. Now he seemed absorbed in examining his powder horn, then filling it from the big horn beside the chimney. He said to her, "I don't know. Indians, anyway. He said the settlers were running down from the north to the Flats. A horseman reached Albany two hours past noon."

He looked up then as he passed the thong of the powder horn over his head.

"Gertrude, you mustn't be worried. There's no real chance the Indians will carry so far as this. And, anyway, we shall have the militia at the bridge."

"I'm not worried."

"Good girl. If you get lonely, go over to the brick house. It's like a fort and Mother has guns for the negroes."

"I won't go over there." She saw the look cross his face. "Unless there are Indians."

He knew how she felt about the Widow Van

Alstyne. The older woman made no bones about telling him what she thought of Gertrude, either— "a black-haired Palatine wench with no 'Van' to her name."

"Give me a kiss, Gertrude."

He put one arm round his wife and kissed her mouth. She had both arms round his neck. The children watched them with interest. It was not usual for their parents to behave so.

Then Van Aernam's voice battered through the wall. "Teunis! It's wet as the ocean out here. Come on!"

"Coming," shouted Teunis in his great voice. He could roar like a bull when he wanted. "Remember, Gertrude. I'll send a man if the Indians go by us. But they'll never get so far."

He had opened the door now. The wind swept past his stout legs to set the candles swaying. Outside the noise of rain and wind-whipped trees was a living sound. The two horses looked all shining, like metal beasts, and Van Aernam, sitting one stoutly, dripped all

around his hat brim.

"We're late already now," he said. "But I don't blame you. Here get up." The children saw his eyes and teeth white under his hat. "It's been a long time since the French were in the valley. But they won't come this far. And if they do, we'll blast the breeches off them."

Teunis had mounted and swung the mare away from the stoop. The two splashed off through the rain. The darkness seemed to come down like the black cover of a closing book to hide them. Gertrude stood for a moment staring after them. Then she leaned against the door to close it, and the wind swept her skirt back from her legs.

Trudy said, "Indians don't wear breeches."

"No," said Gertrude, absently. "That's just a way of talking."

"I think they must feel cold in winter."

Edward said scornfully, "You talk too much, Trudy." He kept watching his mother. He wanted to say that he would look after her; but he felt shy of saying anything to her after the way she had kissed his father.

She said, suddenly, "Time for bed."

Trudy began her usual objections.

"I don't want to go to bed."

"Why not?"

"It's windy, Mama."

"That's nothing."

"I want to sleep with you, Mama."

"You go right up, now," Gertrude said evenly. "No nonsense."

II: IN THE LOFT

✦ ✦ ✦ ✦ ✦

THE two children slept together in the loft room, under the roof, where the smoked hams made a scent in the darkness. On nights when there were stars or a low moon beyond the gable window, they could see the hams, white in their flannel wrappings, like French soldiers in white uniform coats, marching single file. But with the candle Gertrude carried in her hand to give them light, the hams were hams only, and the dark bunches of herbs flanking them were not St. Francis Indians, but boneset, and camomile, and rhubarb.

The loft was warm from the all-day fire in the chimney that passed back of the low bedstead—rising out of the floor boards and penetrating the roof. Above the roof the wind hooted softly in the chimney mouth; the sound brought a sense of the cold and wet beyond the thickness of roof-board and shingle.

The two children undressed quickly, scuffing off their shoes, one each side of the low bedstead. "That isn't neat, Trudy." But Trudy was already wriggling her plump body into the nightgown and dropping on round knees and rattling off her prayers.

Edward was slower, more methodical. He put an ending line for Father, on his prayer, hoping his mother would take notice of it.

She said, "Poor Papa, he must be wet." She pulled the blankets over them. Her hands had a clean buttery smell from the churning she had done that afternoon. Edward smelled it when she came round to his side of the bed. She kissed him swiftly and hard, and then mechanically sang the familiar nursery rhyme as she straightened up to take the candle off the chest.

"Trip a trop a troenje;
De varken en de boenjen."

"Up and down on a little throne;
The pigs are in the beans."

Her voice under the low roof was soft and sweet. Her dark hair took inky shadows from the candle flame, and the long fingers, hardened by her work, shaped themselves to his cheek.

"Good night, sleep well."

"Mama, are the French coming here?"

"No. Papa is waiting. He will not let them get by, if they come even so far as the bridge."

Trudy was already asleep, like a yellowhaired woodchuck, round and fat, burrowing down in the feather tick.

"You aren't afraid, Edward."

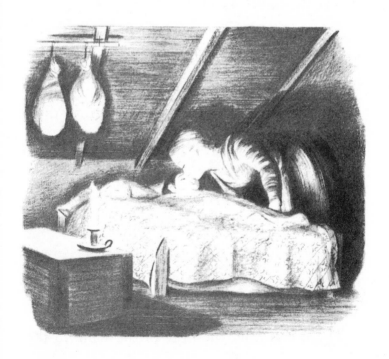

"No, Mama. Are you afraid?"

"No, Edward."

"If the Indians come, call me, Mama. I'll come down and help."

"Yes, Edward."

Gertrude went down the steps one at a time, softly. A moment arrived when just her head and shoulders showed, the smooth line of her throat disappearing into the wide neck of her home-spun dress. The light of the candle shone upward against her face. She stopped for an instant to look back towards the bed, brown-eyed and tender. Then the light grew dim, picking out faintly a square of the roof boards. It went out with a soft sound of her breath. Her feet passed over the floor below.

Edward listened intently. Tonight her clear voice was not answering his father; there was no reassuring laughter from his deep voice to be shut off by the closing of the bedroom door.

There was only the note of the wind in the

chimney and the feeling of it on the roof, like a hand pressed down out of darkness. It was easy to think of it passing through the wet woods, rocking the bare branches where only the beech trees had leaves left to shake.

The gable window remained dark, and the hams along the roof tree remained invisible, but Edward could see them in his mind's eye, like white-coated soldiers, in single file, marching towards the bed.

III: THE SMALL FIELDS

✦ ✦ ✦ ✦ ✦

IN THE morning it was clear, with the wind still blowing, and white clouds in a blue sky moving loftily above the Helderbergs. The two cows, after Gertrude had milked them, lowed along the bank of the Hunger Kill, which had risen too high for them to cross. The land sloping upward from the low stoop was sopping wet, and the narrow road that led to the Palatine road by the corner of Widow Van Alstyne's brick house was a muddy brown brook. The bean vines, leafless, holding only a few ungathered pods, were like damp skeletons of the garden.

Gertrude looked northward as she came in with the milking pail, and the house seemed solitary in an abandoned world. She had had a restless night; it was seldom that her husband had been away overnight—three times since they had been married, she could name each one—but those times it was business in Albany that had kept him away, settling the rent with Patroon Van Rensselaer, or looking up a slave for his mother. He had never stayed out before on militia duty.

A line of smoke, snatched from the chimney by the wind, showed her that Edward was down and had freshened the fire. She thought quickly that with a son it was not as if she were alone. There was Trudy also, of course; but Trudy was too young to notice things.

She wondered whether Teunis would get

back that night. She wondered whether he had any more news of the French and Indians. There never was any definite word of them until the raid was over. Not even when they had burned Schenectady in 1690 had any word of the raid reached Albany until Simon Schemmerhoorn had ridden into town early the next morning. She felt afraid. Their fields were so small in all these woods. An Indian might walk onto the stoop before they were aware of his presence on the farm, if they were indoors at the time. She made up her mind abruptly to keep outside as much as she could all day.

She did not want the children to be frightened, so she talked to them all through their breakfast of corn mush and milk about how the cows were frightened by the water. Every now and then they could hear the distracted bellowing of the two foolish animals striding up and down the shore of the Kill. As if they did not have grass enough on this side! It made the children laugh. The sound of the laughing children made the kitchen seem secure and Gertrude laughed with them, merrily, until Edward asked whether he should take the butter over to Grandmother Van Alstyne.

Gertrude said, "No," suddenly and firmly, so that he stared at her for a long time, and she made a lame explanation of wanting him around the farm to help her with the wood, since Teunis was away.

He said, "Grandmother will be angry if she doesn't get her butter, Mama."

"She can send Tom over to get it." Tom was the widow's head negro.

Trudy asked, "Why haven't we any slaves, Mama?"

Gertrude explained that all the place really belonged to Teunis, so that Grandmother's slaves actually were theirs; but as Grandmother became so cross at the idea of leaving the brick house, they preferred to build their own house and live by themselves.

Trudy said she wished to live in the big house. "Why don't you make Grandma live here, then?"

"One has to be nice to old people."

"Anyone knows that," Edward said to Trudy. "Why don't we all take the butter over together, Mama?"

"No. I am going to stay here, and so are you, Edward."

She acted flustered again. After a while, Edward asked, "Are there Indians in the woods, Mama?"

"No, I don't think so. Papa would send us word if there were. There is nothing to be worried about, Edward."

IV: INDIAN FIRES

✦ ✦ ✦ ✦ ✦

JOHN MYNDERSE rode down after lunch, carrying his musket in his hands, balancing it on the withers of his bright bay horse. He called for Gertrude to come out, and she closed the door behind her so that the children, looking through the window, could not hear what was said. The sun was warmer now and the wind was dying down and the bay horse rested his hip while Mynderse talked down to their mother. She tilted her face up at him, looking young and small and worried.

"Teunis says to tell you everything is all right. But the French Indians are burning the upper settlements. People have been killed. They have sent a company from Albany to the Flats. The company will stop them all right, Gertrude."

"What are you doing?"

"Teunis wanted to let you know, that is all. I am riding over to Van Epps' and to my own place. But Teunis thinks maybe you had better go over to the big house." Mynderse looked down at her. "He won't get back tonight either, probably."

"Tell him not to worry about us. We are fine." He looked away from her as she

squared her shoulders. "Tell me, does he want anything?"

Mynderse shook his head. "Yes, I forgot. He wants his schnapps in the wood flask."

"All right," she said. "Doesn't he want any food? Bread?"

"He didn't say, but we could use food. There are quite a lot of us."

"Just a minute." She flew into the house to get the schnapps. "Get the big loaf of bread, Trudy. And you get the ham, the big one at the end, Edward."

In a moment they had the food ready for Mynderse. He put the flask over his shoulder and the loaf in his bag and took the ham in his arm. "Just like my baby," he said, grinning at the children, and they laughed soberly.

They watched him clop away up the road, leaving deep tracks in the mud, and Edward said, "Mynderse does not ride like Father. He is like a flour sack sitting on a horse."

"You must not say such things about Mynderse. He is very kind."

Trudy clapped her hands and said, "The Indians don't wear breeches!" She sang it. "The Indians don't wear breeches. Oh, the Indians don't wear breeches," till she was hushed up and was sullen and went around muttering something. Edward finally asked her what she said, and she answered in a deep voice, "Bergom op Zoom!"

He looked up at the Spanish Gun at once. It seemed like a cannon with the afternoon light shining through the window along the whole length of it. He thought they need not be afraid with that in the house.

Gertrude said, "Let us go out for a little walk."

"Where to?"

"Oh, just for some air. And then we can get in the cows."

They went out, and to please Trudy, Mama

allowed her to wear the old shawl, so that she looked like a comical dwarf woman with fat legs. The children chattered all the way along and Gertrude had no trouble in leading them up the knoll beyond the garden. It was quite a high rise of ground. From the top of it one could see out clear into the north and east.

The sun was half way down and the west wind, though it was much milder, was like a stream against their cheeks. The children saw the smoke as soon as Gertrude did. It was a leaning cloud, far in the north. They could see it plain against the pale horizon.

"Is it far away?" the children asked.

"Yes." Gertrude was straining her eyes. She tried to imagine where it came from. She thought it was much nearer than the north settlements. Near the Flats, she thought, since it showed so distinctly.

"Is it a big fire, Mama?"

"Yes, I think so."

"I want to see it!" said Trudy. "I want."

"It is too far. It is time to be getting back to the house."

Edward was silent. They walked down together with the wind cold in their faces and saw the cows by the creek.

"Come," cried Gertrude, "we must get them in."

"I'll get them," said Edward.

"No, we'll all get them. Hurry."

Trudy ran, waving a stick and screeching, "Bergom op Zoom!" but Edward kept watching his mother. He knew now that she was afraid.

"Are the Indians near?"

"Not very." She made her voice sound calm. Luckily the cows were eager to be brought in.

They fastened them and went into the house. Then Trudy was sent to wash her face and Gertrude called Edward.

She looked pale and serious.

"I think the Indians are quite near, Edward. You must not go out any more."

"Why don't we go over to Grandmother's?"

"It is better here." She thought of an excuse. "If Papa comes back, he would want to find us at home, Edward."

V: LOADING THE GUN

✦ ✦ ✦ ✦ ✦

SHE had thought out her course while getting the cows. It was better to stay. Their place was away from the main road, and raiders would be more likely to know and see the brick house. She knew that she could not help the grandmother, who would not want her help in any case, and she thought only of the best way to keep the children safe. To stay seemed the best way to her. Trudy's shouting had given her an idea for defending the house, for it seemed to her that if the Indians came they would not arrive as far as this except in small groups.

"Edward, I want you to be a brave boy and do everything I tell you."

"Yes, Mama."

"Would you be afraid to fire Great-Grandfather's gun?"

Edward looked up at the Spanish matchlock, all the great length of it, and said with a white, excited face, "No, Mama. But I can't hold it."

"I can fix that," she said. "But you must do exactly what I say."

She went over to the fireplace and mounted a stool and took down the huge gun. It was beginning to grow dusky in the Kill Valley already, and the kitchen had turned gray and

shadowy. She lit a candle.

"Fetch the big powder horn."

She had no idea how much powder to put into the gun, but she doubled what seemed to her a musket charge. She wadded it down with a piece of writing paper, standing at the end of the barrel and pushing the rod, because of the length of the gun.

"It hasn't any bullets," Edward said.

"See if there are some with Papa's mold."

Edward found two. They rolled down the barrel with a faint rattling sound. Gertrude was not satisfied. She leaned the gun on a chair and told Edward not to let Trudy touch it. Trudy came in at that moment and as soon as she saw the gun she stopped dead. For once she was speechless.

Gertrude rummaged, finding some horseshoe nails and some small pebbles and two brass buttons. She rammed them all down and wadded them hard. Then she got Teunis's axe and chopped out a corner of the blind of the window at the left of the stoop door.

With Edward helping, she dragged the table
to the window and then lifted the gun onto it,
and with all her flatirons propped the gun so
that it pointed to the missing corner of the
blind, straight out onto the steps of the stoop.
She bolted the blinds then, not only of that

window but of the other windows also, and dropped the bar over the shed door.

She had become very silent in doing these things, and so had the children watching her. Edward trembled a little when she drew a stool up to the table and told him to get onto it. Then she primed the gun and set the candle beside it.

Seeing the whole thing complete, Trudy suddenly said with great acuteness, in a loud voice, "Bergom op Zoom!"

"Hush," said Gertrude. "Trudy, you must not talk. You must play on Mama's and Papa's bed." She made a doll out of a handkerchief and got a large lump of maple sugar and some of the silver spoons and put them and Trudy together on the bed, leaving the door open so that she would not be frightened. The little girl settled down in delight on the big bed and held her doll up so she could see, and whispered, "Bergom op Zoom," very softly.

VI: EDWARD'S ORDERS

✦ ✦ ✦ ✦ ✦

GERTRUDE went back to her son, thinking how young he was to have so much to do. "Edward, you must listen to me."

"Yes, Mama."

"I am going outside to look for Indians. If they come, I shall call your name, ATEOORD! Loud as I can. Then you must touch the candle to this place."

"Yes, Mama," he said eagerly.

"You must not do it before."

"No, Mama."

"You must not touch anything until I call your name. If I call Teunis, or Mynderse, or Uncle Sylvanus, you must not touch anything. But when I call ATEOORD, then what will you do?"

Edward reached for the candle.

"No, NO! You must not touch anything."

"I wasn't going to," he said in a low, indignant voice. He moved his hand through the gesture of touching the priming. She leaned down from behind and put her arms around him and kissed him.

"Good, brave boy."

He sat rigidly still. He looked small and white and dark-eyed. There was a hole in the knee of his stocking—she had meant to mend it that day.

"What do you do?" she asked again.

He repeated her instructions carefully and accurately.

"You are a smart boy," she said. "Do you know, even Papa has never fired that Spanish Gun?"

"Yes, I know." His voice shook a little. "Will it make an awful noise, Mama?"

"Yes, it will scare the Indians, and Papa will be so proud."

"Where are you going?"

"Just outside, Edward, to watch for the Indians."

"Not far?"

"No, I'll be near. Remember, you must not even move from the stool."

"No, Mama."

She looked at him once, then at Trudy; then, making her face serene as she could, she took up her shawl and a basket and went out of the house, closing the door upon them.

VII: INDIANS ON THE FARM

✦ ✦ ✦ ✦ ✦

SHE had taken the basket to pick beans into.
The pods remaining were worthless, but she
wanted to have an excuse to stay out. Any
raider coming must not be made suspicious. She
had thought of picking the bean pods because
she had noticed them early that morning.

It had seemed to her as if the whole day had been made of pieces that had fitted together suddenly when silly little Trudy began screeching "Bergom op Zoom" after the cows.

Now, walking up to the garden patch, across the wind, she wondered whether she had not been acting hysterically. She had put Edward under a strain that no boy only ten years old ought to have. She had left him frightened, cold, with his resolution to be brave. She seemed to see him sitting there by the table at the end of the monstrous gun, listening and listening. But she knew that she could have done nothing else, unless she took them to Widow Van Alstyne's. As for that, she could still persuade herself that she had been right in considering her own house the safer place.

Twilight had stretched across to the Helderbergs when she came among the bean vines. She began picking pods into her basket, slowly, one at a time, fumbling with her hands

in the cold wind, and watching the woods unceasingly. It would soon be too dark to be able to see the woods. There was only a pale light to show the rolling tops of the hills. There was no light at all to the north now, and the night was a visible blackness in the sky.

So that Edward might not feel too deserted, now and then she sang, her voice carrying away from her lips along the wind. She hoped he could hear her.

> *"Trip a trop a troenje;*
> *De varken en de boenjen."*

"Up and down on a little throne;
The pigs are in the beans."

The wind seemed to be falling still lower with the failing light. Now and then she could hear the water running in the Hunger Kill below.

The widow's was a brick house, stout as a fort. As she thought of it, Gertrude turned in that direction and saw a rise of flames through the branches. She had been right, then. Van Alstyne's was afire. The wind was dying and the flames sprang high. Silence had come into their own little valley. She understood suddenly that the Indians had got by. They were in the Helderbergs. Where Teunis and his men could be she did not know. It was too late for him to help her now. But if she had been right all the way through, maybe she would not need him, after all. Maybe the Indians would not come along the Hunger Kill to find their house.

It was then that she saw the Indians.

VIII: "ATEOORD!"

✦ ✦ ✦ ✦ ✦

THERE were five of them, dark shapes on the road, coming from the brick house. They hardly looked like men, the way they moved. They were trotting, stooped over, first one and then another coming up, like dogs sifting up to the scent of food. Gertrude felt her heart pound hard; then it seemed to stop altogether.

She realized that they had not seen her. They were heading straight for the house, leaving the road now, so that their feet would make no sound in the mud. Her heart started to beat again. But her hands were stiff as she grasped the basket and stepped from the bean poles into the open. She made a pretense of seeing them for the first time. She stopped stock still, facing them, making herself count five. Then she ran for the house.

She must not lose her head. She must not run so fast as to outdistance them, for then she would have to wait on the stoop. They should be right behind her, only a step away from her.

She glanced back over her shoulder to see them loping along in long strides. They did not seem to cover the ground fast, yet they were already well up on her. She could see the feathers in the upstanding scalplocks of the leading three. She screamed, "Teunis!" and ran for the house with all her might. She had not meant to let them get so close. The road was muddy and the footing treacherous. If they

overtook her before she reached the stoop it would be no good at all. She would be killed, Edward and Trudy, the house burned.

She called, "Sylvanus! Van Aernam! Mynderse!" She had not thought before how utterly she had put her trust in Edward.

Coming down the slope of ground, the Indians closed in with unbelievable rapidity.

Gertrude was a good runner. But she had never run as fast as this. She could hear the pounding of their feet over her own and the hammering of the blood in her head. But she kept her feet and ran up the steps onto the stoop, and shouted, "ATEOORD!"

Then a flashing pain entered her shoulder at the back and she was flung against the door. She knew the Indians had thrown a tomahawk at

her. A second, missing her, entered the door beside her face. She turned about weakly to see them springing onto the steps, their heads faintly lit from candlelight shining through the chink in the blind, their faces painted red and yellow and white, and the silver rings swinging outward from their ears.

A tremendous flash, a roar that shook the stoop under her, and a choking cloud of smoke removed them. She saw the leader cave in over his own knees and the next two flung back on their shoulders. She saw nothing else at all, but she knew that Edward had touched off the Spanish Gun.

IX: FIRING THE GUN

✦ ✦ ✦ ✦ ✦

WHEN Edward touched the candle to the priming of the Spanish Gun he felt so cold that he could hardly move. He had heard his mother running down the road and had heard her shouts for his father and Uncle Sylvanus, now dead for a long time, for Van Aernam and

Mynderse, and then he had heard the running feet of the Indians behind her. He could see nothing through the chink. Outside it was black dark. He did not even touch the candle then, but he fastened his eyes on the priming and moved his hand to the candle, ready to take it up.

Then she was calling, "Ateoord!" and he heard the tomahawk drive into the door as he laid the flame down on the gunpowder. It fizzed for an instant, smoking out of the priming hole. Then the gun roared, shattering the glass, and the butt, striking him fair in the chest, carried him backward off the stool.

He was not aware of it; he was not aware of anything till he heard Trudy screaming. That woke him up to the fact that he was lying on the floor of the kitchen with the Spanish Gun like a log on top of him. He was puzzled to find the dead candle in his hand, for there was light enough to see Trudy.

He managed to wriggle out from under the gun, but the pain in his chest was so great that he could do nothing except crawl on hands and knees to the door. It was open. The light came from there. He crawled through to see the stoop ablaze, his mother lying on it like a dead person, and little Trudy desperately lugging at the handle of an Indian axe fast in their mother's shoulder. For an instant he could not take it in. Then he realized that the fire was almost to his mother's skirt.

He ordered Trudy to let go of the axe and help him drag their mother off the stoop. It was lucky she was so small. It was lucky, also, that the stoop was low, for they had to tumble her over the edge. In her fall the axe was dislodged enough for Edward to pull it forth himself.

"Is Mother killed?" asked Trudy.

Edward did not know, but he said she was alive. He made Trudy take off her shirt and he stuffed it into the open wound as well as he was able. There was plenty of light now. The flames from the stoop were already climbing up the walls.

The light went out into the yard, picking out the pools of rain water like shining eyes. They showed, too, the tumbled bodies of three dead Indians.

Edward tried to drag his mother away from

them; but he could not move her. He sent Trudy inside to get blankets, telling her to hurry. She brought them from the bedroom, together with her handkerchief doll. She said gravely, "I didn't want it to get burned to death."

"No," said Edward. He thought Trudy had done well. He looked down at the dead Indians, thinking how big they were. Then he remembered the Spanish Gun.

He could not leave it there. Though he felt better, it was hard for him to walk, and harder yet to drag out the ponderous gun. But he managed it at last, taking it out the back door and lugging it round the house. The stock left a furrow in the mud.

Then he and Trudy sat down together between their mother and the dead Indians, watching the house burn, and kept warm by its heat.

Trudy grew sleepy, after a while, and lost her

interest in the dead Indians. She was no longer afraid of them. She teetered toward Edward and leaned down into his lap. Her head struck the lock of the gun and she said, "Bergom op Zoom."

"Yes," Edward said. "Great-Grandfather Dygert brought it from Bergom op Zoom to the wild America."

He was glad he had remembered to save it. Such a wonderful gun to show *his* grandchildren, maybe.

X: THE MILITIA RETURN

✛ ✛ ✛ ✛ ✛

TEUNIS, riding in with half a dozen militia-men, found them so: Gertrude still uncon-scious. Trudy asleep, and Edward sitting up with the gun across his knees, the bell mouth pointing at the three dead Indian bodies.

On their way in, the men had found the barns burned at the brick house and Grandmother Van Alstyne and her slaves barricaded, refusing even then to come out.

And in the creek valley they had found another Indian crippled and had killed him. But now while Teunis picked up Gertrude, the others just sat their horses and stared from Edward to the dead Indians.

"They sneaked by us," Mynderse said. "Who shot them, Edward?"

"I did. With the Spanish Gun," said Edward.

"You've killed more than all the rest of us put together!" Mynderse exclaimed, and he picked up the gun and hefted it. But before he could say anything more, plump Trudy woke up suddenly.

"Bergom op Zoom!" she said, pointing solemnly at Edward.

Walter D. Edmonds was born in the small town of Boonville in upper New York State, the setting for many of his stories. He attended St. Paul's School in New Hampshire and Choate in Connecticut, and received his A. B. degree at Harvard. His historical novel, DRUMS ALONG THE MOHAWK, has become a modern classic, and THE MATCHLOCK GUN was awarded the Newbery Medal in 1942 as "the most distinguished contribution to American literature for children."

The scene of most of Walter Edmonds' writing has been the colorful Mohawk Valley and the Black River Canal which he knows so well. "When I started to write it was natural to start writing about the place and people I was most familiar with," he said. "New York State happens to be unique in representing practically the whole history of this country within its own boundaries." Mr. Edmonds lived in Concord, Massachusetts in his later life and passed away in 1998.